LOOKING FOR CLUES

by Judith Brand
illustrated by Kevin Rechin

⧄Harcourt

Orlando   Boston   Dallas   Chicago   San Diego

Visit *The Learning Site!*

www.harcourtschool.com

Nolan opens his eyes. It's a beautiful day. He pulls back the sheet and jumps onto the floor.

"Hello, Roxann! Get up!"
Nolan scolds. "Let's ask Dad
to go to the park. I want to
be a nature detective and find
animal clues."

"Look over here," says Nolan. "Something walked here not long ago. These are big footprints! They show only two toes."

"These animals have webbed feet," says Roxann. "Mom told me that webbed feet help water birds swim. Which bird made these?"

"Look over at these tracks,"
says Roxann. "They look like
little hands and feet. What
animal has paws like that? I'll
make a sketch."

"I know it has paws that can hold things," says Nolan.

"This animal is usually busy at night," adds Dad.

"Something crawled over this old road," says Nolan. "But it left no footprints. It left a trail."

"I know who!" yells Roxann.

"Look at all these holes," says Nolan. "Do animals eat wood?"

"Not usually," says Dad. "But this one does."

"Let's both look at these
seeds," Roxann says to Nolan.
"They also have holes.
Many animals eat seeds.
Which animal opened these?"

"That cold soda was good!"
says Roxann.
    "Let's clean up," says Dad.
"Pick up every piece."

"Both nests and eggs are clues about birds," Dad says. "Look at the shape of the nest and the speckled eggs."

"A feather is also a clue," says Nolan. "What bird has blue feathers? What bird has speckled eggs?"

"We'll find out," says Roxann.

"Let's go home and say hello to Mom," says Nolan. "We can also show her the clues."

"I told you we could find out who ate this," says Roxann. "A squirrel did!"

deer

snail

termite

duck

squirrel

raccoon

Stellar's
jay

Roxann and Nolan found
the animals that left each clue.
Did you?